A Lake in Pixie Hollow

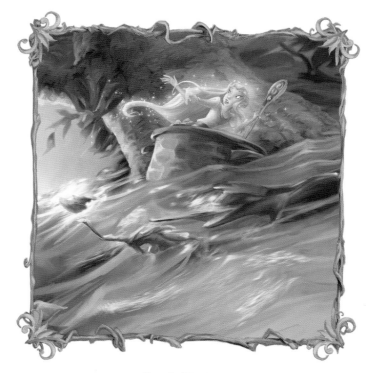

-»» Book Eight «-

Disney PRESS
New York

D1409969

Illustrated by the Disney Storybook Artists
Designed by Deborah Boone

Printed in China

First Edition
3 5 7 9 10 8 6 4 2

ISBN 978-1-4231-2936-3
T425-2382-5-11129

For more Disney Press fun,
visit www.disneybooks.com

Early one morning, Rani hurried down the stairs of the
Home Tree, on her way to see her friend Tinker Bell.
Rani wasn't looking where she was going, so she didn't
notice anything unusual, until suddenly . . .

Splash!

Rani looked down. She was standing in water. A teapot
and three cups floated by. "Oh, my!" Rani exclaimed. "The
dishes are floating away!"

"The dishes aren't the only thing floating away!" a nearby
fairy cried.

Rani looked over and saw Dulcie, a baking-talent fairy,
bobbing across the water in a large stockpot. "All of Pixie
Hollow is flooded!" Dulcie declared.

Just then, they heard someone outside cry, "Help!"

"It sounds like someone's in trouble!" Rani said. She leaped into Dulcie's pot, and the two fairies paddled outside.

They saw Lily, a garden-talent fairy. She was trying to rescue a nest of chicks that had fallen into the water.

"The nest is too heavy!" Lily cried to the fairies. "Can you help me pull it in?"

Quickly, Rani and Dulcie got behind Lily. Soon they had pulled the chicks to safety.

Everyone breathed a sigh of relief.

Rani noticed Dulcie's stockpot floating atop the water. It reminded her of something. . . . "I completely forgot—I have to go see Tink!" Rani exclaimed. "Dulcie, can I borrow your pot and spoon?"

"Oh, sure," Dulcie said. "My wings are nearly dry now. Soon, I'll be able to fly again."

Rani climbed into the pot.

"There's a dent in one of the handles," Dulcie called as Rani began to paddle away. "Would you ask Tink to—"

"Fix it? She'd love to!" Rani waved and paddled off.

Soon Rani arrived at Tink's workshop and went inside. As she did, three little minnows followed her.

"These fish keep trying to get into my pots and pans!" Tink exclaimed. "Every time I open the door, they jump in."

"What about a decoy?" Rani suggested.

Tink thought this was a wonderful idea, so she dangled a shiny spoon under the water. Just then, Spring, a message-talent fairy, arrived.

"Beck needs your help!" she told Rani. "Climb aboard and I'll take you to her."

"Oh, Tink, I almost forgot!" Rani called back as they paddled away. "I brought you Dulcie's stockpot. It has a dent in the handle."

Tink smiled. "You always bring the best presents, Rani," she said.

On their way to see Beck, Spring and Rani spotted Terence, a fairy-dust-talent sparrow man. He looked worried. "The fairy dust is all wet!" Terence told them. "It could take days to dry out. Until then, no one will be able to fly!"

"That is terrible news," Spring said sadly.

Suddenly, a group of water-talent fairies in leaf boats appeared. They began to sing as they dipped their oars in the new lake.

One of the water fairies reached out to touch the water and a fountain shot up where her fingers had been. Other water-talent fairies began to set off their own fountains. They were happy to see so much water.

And the other fairies were overjoyed, too. "Of course!" cried Terence. "We can use the water fairies' boats to get around!"

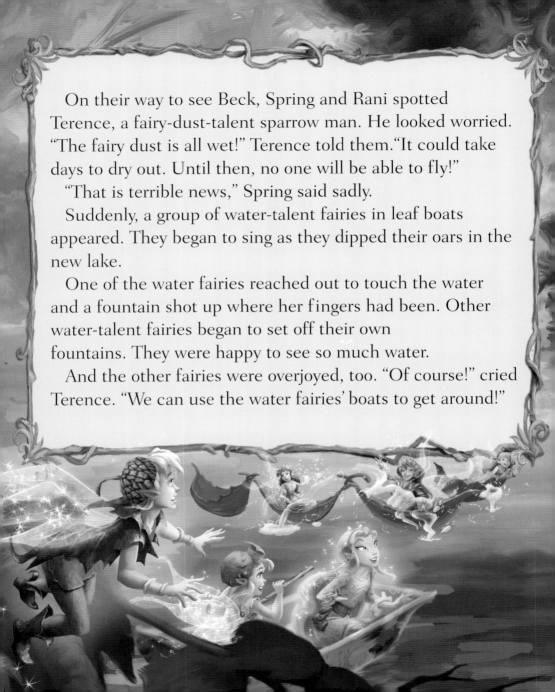

While Terence and the water fairies delivered the leaf boats, Rani hurried off to look for Beck. She found her in the Home Tree lobby, trying to coax three chipmunks up the stairs.

"Beck, what are you doing?" Rani asked.

"The chipmunks have nowhere to live!" Beck cried. "Their house is flooded."

"So you brought them here?" Rani asked.

"They have to go somewhere," Beck insisted. "They can stay in my room. Rani, you're a water-talent fairy," she went on. "Can't you do something about all of this water?"

"I don't know where it's coming from," Rani admitted.

Two days later, Pixie Hollow was still flooded. But no one seemed to mind as much. Although they still couldn't fly, the fairies were getting around quite well. The animal-talent fairies had asked some spiders to weave walkways above the water. The garden-talent fairies had moved their favorite plants to a patio high in the Home Tree. And nearly all the fairies had become experts at leaf-boating.

"Hello, Spring," Rani said as she pulled up next to Spring's leaf boat. "Beautiful day, isn't it?"

"It is!" said Spring. "You know, Rani, I thought this flood was awful at first. But it really isn't so bad, since everyone pitched in to help."

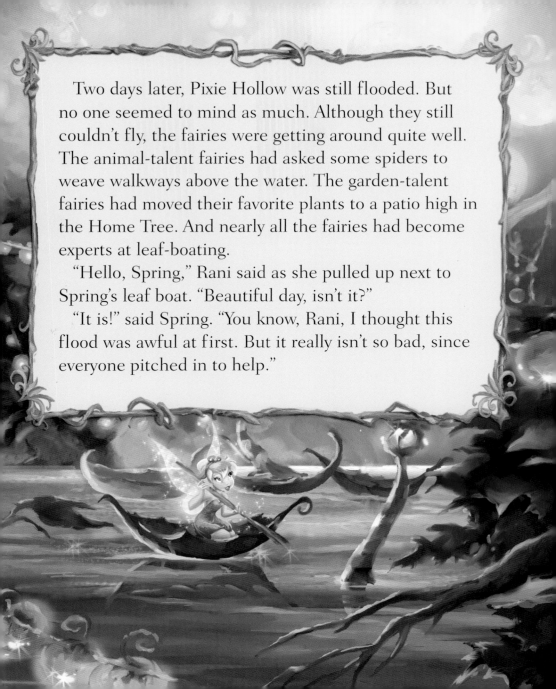

"Rani! Rani!" someone called suddenly.

Turning, Rani saw Beck riding on the back of a turtle. "I just went to visit my friends the squirrels," Beck said breathlessly. "They told me what is causing the flood!"

"What is it?" Rani asked.

"Beavers have built a dam across Havendish Stream. It's backed up all the way to Pixie Hollow," Beck said. "I'd go talk to them, but it's too far by leaf boat. And my turtle friend wants to get back to his home."

"Brother Dove can take us there," suggested Rani.

Rani whistled for Brother Dove, who came at once. The two fairies climbed onto his back. A moment later, they were soaring above the trees.

"Look!" Rani cried suddenly. "There it is!" Almost directly below them, the fairies could see the beaver dam. Water had risen over the banks of Havendish Stream and flooded the forest all around.

Brother Dove set Beck and Rani down on top of the dam.

"Hello!" Beck called in Beaver. Soon three brown heads poked out of the water right in front of her.

Beck chattered to the beavers in their own language, explaining the fairies' problem. The beavers chattered back.

"They say they don't want to move," Beck told Rani. "It took them a long time to find the perfect spot."

Rani thought for a moment. "Tell them that I know a better spot," she urged. "Just up the stream. There's a waterfall . . . and lots of trees."

Beck turned to the beavers and told them what Rani had said.

The beavers were silent for a moment. Then they smacked their tails loudly against the water.

"They say yes!" Beck cried.

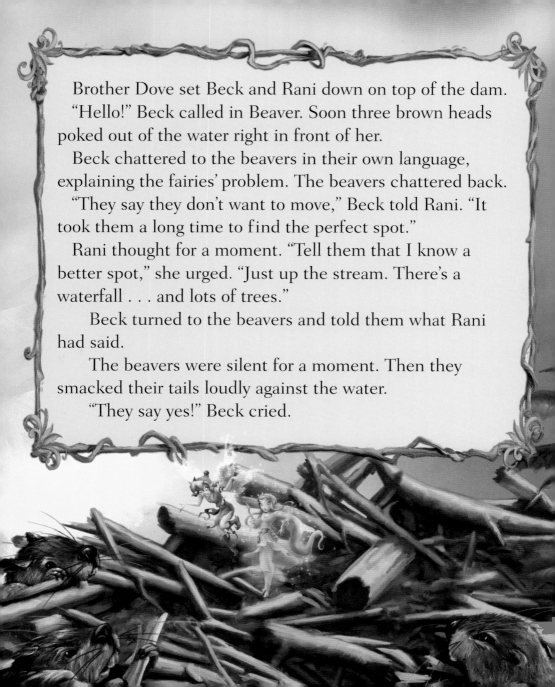

The next day, the beavers moved their dam. Soon the waters receded. The sun shone down on brilliant green grass. Blue and purple flowers peeked up around tree roots.

Rani found Tink standing next to her leaf boat. She looked a little sad.

"What's wrong, Tink?" Rani asked. "Aren't you happy? Pixie Hollow is back to normal!"

"I guess," Tink said with a little sigh. "But I was just getting used to the water."

"You know," Rani said thoughtfully, "that's just what Dulcie said. And Spring has been missing her leaf boat, too."

"I even miss those minnows," said Tink.

The next day, Rani arrived at Tink's workshop. "Come on!" she cried happily. "And bring your shiniest spoon!"

Rani led Tink to a spot next to Havendish Stream. It had been transformed into a fairy-sized lake! Some fairies zipped around in leaf boats while others waded at the edge. As Tink and Rani approached the water, a little school of fish swam up.

"My minnows!" cried Tink. She dangled her spoon down into the water and laughed as the fish gathered around her.

With the lake to remind them, the fairies would never forget the flood and how they all worked together.